Tots and the Brass Band

Written by Ragdoll

Illustrated by Penny Lane

A Ragdoll Production for Central Independent Television

Hippo

Scholastic Children's Books,
7-9 Pratt Street, London NW1 0AE
A division of Scholastic Publications Ltd
London-New York-Toronto-Sydney-Auckland

Published in the UK by Scholastic Publications Ltd, 1995
Text copyright © Ragdoll 1995
Illustrations copyright © Penny Lane 1995

Original script Robin Stevens, Anne Wood, Andrew Davenport.
Text adapted by Jack Ousbey
Design of Tots - TV puppets and house
copyright © Ragdoll Productions (UK) Ltd 1993
Central logo copyright © Central Independent Television plc 1989
Based on the Central Independent Television series produced by Ragdoll Productions

ISBN: 0 590 55942 7

Typeset by Rapid Reprographics
Printed in Great Britain by Bath Press Colourbooks, Glasgow

10 9 8 7 6 5 4 3 2 1

All was quiet in the secret house where the Tots lived. Tilly woke up first.

"Bonjour, Tots," she said.

"Good morning, Tilly," said Tiny.

"Tots," said Tom, "I think something interesting is going to happen today. I have a feeling, I have."

Tiny took the magic bag from its peg and they were ready to go adventuring out.

"Eee-aw," said Donkey as they went through the garden.

"What will we see today?" sang the Tots, "What will we see?"

"Peek a boo," said Furryboo.

As the Tots walked down the lane they could see a crowd gathering on the village green, and from far away they heard the sound of music.

"What's that noise?" asked Tiny.

"C'est musique," said Tilly.

"That is a musical noise, that is," said Tom.

TEA
+
BUNS

The Tots hid behind a wall and then peeped over.
There were the villagers, smiling and nodding and
looking towards the church. Round the corner came a
band.

7

"Wow," said Tiny, "look at their brilliant uniforms."
"And Tots," said Tom, "see how their instruments shine in the sun."

"C'est magnifique," said Tilly. "J'aime le trombone, Tiny."

"I like the cymbals best," said Tiny.

"Actually, Tots," said Tom, "I like the drum and the euphonium."

9

The musicians were now sitting down to practise, and the Tots found a hiding place next to the big drum. The band struck up and the Tots were amazed when they heard the tune the band was playing.

"It's our song," said Tom. "The one we sing in our house."

"C'est la chanson, *Un, Deux, Trois*," said Tilly. As the band played on, the Tots joined in.

Listen to the marching band,
Listen to the music.
Hear the big euphonium –
Ooom-pah-pah.
Listen to the big bass drum,
Listen to the cymbals.
Hear the big euphonium –
Ooom-pah-pah.

Just then, Tilly picked up the drumstick and banged on the big bass drum – Boom—Boom—De—Boom went the drum.

"Stop," said the bandmaster. "Someone's playing
wrong notes. We'll have a break for a cup of tea now.
Let's hope we get it right next time."

Tom couldn't stop giggling. "That was a little bit
naughty of you, Tilly, that was."

"Look," said Tiny, "they have left all their
instruments on the chairs."

Tom and Tiny went to look at the euphonium.

"I'm going to blow a nice, musical noise through this, I am," said Tom. "You stand just there, Tiny, and listen."

"All right," Tiny said. "I'm listening."

"Ready, then," said Tom. "Here goes."

14

He took a big breath and blew into the euphonium. No sound came out. He took another even bigger breath and tried again.

"Can you hear anything?" he asked.

"Actually, not even the smallest, little sound," said Tiny. "I think I should have a go now."

Tom and Tiny changed places. Tiny breathed in and out for practice, then took a very deep breath and blew with all his strength.

BARoooooooooom—PaaaaaaaaaaH
went the euphonium.

The mighty noise made Tom's head wobble and spin.

"Tiny," gasped Tom, "my poor ears are ringing, they are."

"I must have got it just right," said Tiny. "It was an extra special musical note actually."

Tilly was trying to play the trombone. She could only manage a Wah–Wah sound. Tom and Tiny took hold of the trombone slide and, as Tilly blew, they pushed and pulled.

WaaaaH – aaaaH – Waaaah – aaaaH
went the trombone, making a lovely, moany sound.

The musicians returned and, as the band lined up to march round the village, Tilly said, "Regarde, le sac magique."

19

She put the magic bag on the ground. It jiggled and joggled. The flap opened up, and there, peeping out, were a small drum and some cymbals. Tom put the drum cord round his neck, Tiny strapped on the cymbals, and Tilly took out her own magic flute. As the band marched round the green, the Tots followed on behind, in time to the *One, Two, Three* tune. Tom and Tiny sang as they marched.

Off we go together now
Marching through the village,
Rootle–ti–toot, clangetty-clang–
Barrum, barrum, barrum.
Rat-a-tat tat and oompah-pah
Round and round the village,
Playing the tune we always play –
Barrum, barrum, barrum.

When they marched round the green a second time, the Tots dodged into the lane that led back to the Secret House.

"We've had a good old marching day, today," said Tom.

"We've had a good old marching, singing, blowing, drumming day, actually Tom," said Tiny.

"Oui," said Tilly. "C'était génial."

Just as the Tots were walking up their garden path, Tilly stopped.

"J'ai une idée," she said. "Un concert, dans le jardin."

"What a good idea. A musical concert in the garden," said Tom.

"The only thing is, Tots, we haven't an audience."

"We can be the audience," said Tiny. "When each of us performs, the other two watch."

"That is a brilliant idea, that is, Tiny," said Tom.

The Tots went off to get ready. Tiny went up to the bedroom, Tilly sat in the window seat, and Tom stayed outside. Tiny came down early with a large piece of card and wrote down on it what each of the Tots would be doing at the concert.

When he had finished, he pinned it on Donkey's door. It said:

do not miss today's concert

there will be a musical concert in the garden at 6 o'clock today

1. Tilly will play a french song on the flute

2. Tom will sing and play the drums

3. Tiny will play the cymbals

please do not be late

X + X X
       X

No one was late. Donkey wondered what was going on, and put his head out to watch. Tiny introduced Tilly. The flute song she played was so catchy, Tom and Tiny asked her to play it again and they clapped very hard when she finished.

Tom's drumming turn was a great success. He marched up and down the garden singing –

I am Tom and I'm playing my drum –
Rad-a-dum, rad-a-dum, rad-a-dum.
Please tap your feet when you hear the beat
Of my rad-a-dum, rad-a-dum drum.
Here am I, head held high,
Drumming hard and marching by –
Rad-a-dum, rad-a-dum, rad-a-dum.

At last, it was Tiny's turn. The cymbals clashed and clanged as Tiny danced on top of the cart, whirling this way and that.

Tilly and Tom shouted and laughed, as Tiny went faster and faster, and when he jumped off the cart they all joined in, banging and clanging and chasing round the garden. They ended up in a giggling heap just under Donkey's door.

"Eee-aw," said Donkey.

"He liked our concert," said Tiny.

"So did I," said Tom. "It was a very nice musical event."

"C'était un concert dément," said Tilly.

"You're right," Tiny agreed. "A mad concert from the Tots."

Later the Tots were tired. It was time for bed.
As they went upstairs they heard Donkey
"Eee-aw" goodnight from outside.
   When they were curled up in their beds
they sang – very softly – their Goodnight Song.

We've had some adventures,
some songs and some fun,
It's time now for sleeping,
our busy day's done.
So it's Bonne Nuit, Tilly,
and Sleep Well, Tom.
It's Goodnight Tiny
– and everyone.

And very soon, all was quiet in the Secret House where the Tots lived. And then from somewhere in the rafters Furryboo gave a little "Peek-a-boo."